The Baseball Game

With Lots of Love,

Grandma Diane
and

Grandpa Wally

Library of Congress Cataloging-in-Publication Data

Dobson, Danae.
  The baseball game / Danae Dobson ; illustrated by Karen Loccisano.
    p. cm. — (The Sunny Street Kids' Club ; 3)
  "Word kids!"
  Summary: Connor and his friends worry about facing the three meanest boys at
Hillside Elementary School in a baseball game, but they learn that winning is not as
important as playing fairly.
  ISBN 0–8499–5114–3
  [1. Baseball—Fiction. 2. Bullies—Fiction. 3. Christian life—Fiction.] I. Loccisano,
Karen, ill. II. Title. III. Series: Dobson, Danae. Sunny Street Kids' Club ; 3.
PZ7.D6614Bas   1996
[Fic]—dc20   95–53287
                                                     CIP
                                                       AC

Printed in Hong Kong

96 97 98 99 00 PLP 9 8 7 6 5 4 3 2 1

The Baseball Game

by
Danae Dobson

Illustrated by Karen Loccisano

WORD PUBLISHING
Dallas·London·Vancouver·Melbourne

The Sunny Street Kids' Club gathered at the park after school. Everyone was there—Connor, Matthew, Stephanie, Lauren, and Connor's little brother, Ryan. They were practicing to get ready for their school's big field event on Saturday. It was only two days away.

Connor had signed up his friends to play baseball at two o'clock on Saturday afternoon.

But there was just one problem: They hadn't practiced enough.

Connor called for everyone's attention. "Who wants to be in the outfield?"

"I will!" said Lauren.

"And I'll be the catcher," said Matthew.

Stephanie chose first base, and Ryan second base.

"I guess I'll be the pitcher," added Connor.

Matthew was the first one up to bat. He swung as hard as he could. The ball flew through the air.

"All right!" Connor exclaimed.

Just then, Rusty took off running across the field.
"Hey!" shouted Lauren. "Look out!" Rusty jumped
up and caught the ball in his mouth.

Connor laughed.

"Rusty thinks he's an outfielder!" he said.

"Well, he almost knocked me over," Lauren complained. Connor dragged Rusty across the field by his collar.

"No!" he said, shaking his finger in the dog's face. "Stay here!"

Rusty looked rejected as Connor walked away.

"All right," said Connor. "Who's next?"

Stephanie
stepped up to
the plate. She hit
a ground ball that
bounced over second base.

Once again, Rusty dashed and caught the ball
near second base.

"That does it!" said Lauren, throwing her mitt
on the ground. "How can we practice with Rusty
interfering?"

"I'm sorry," said Connor. "I didn't know this
would happen."

Connor scolded Rusty again and told him to
stay on the sideline.

But the dog wouldn't obey. Every time someone hit the ball, Rusty was right there to catch it.

The children finally gave up and began walking home.

"Connor, I hope you're not going to bring Rusty to the game on Saturday," said Matthew. "Not after what happened this afternoon."

"Of course, I'm going to bring him," said Connor. "He's our club mascot! A mascot should always be at a sporting event."

"But what if he gets in the way again?" asked
Stephanie. "We could lose the game!"

"Not to worry," said Connor. "I'll keep him
tied to the fence so he won't cause any trouble."

Lauren rolled her eyes. "I hope not," she said.

The next day at school, Matthew ran to see his friends after class.

"Did you guys read the sign-up sheet today?" he asked. "Ronnie, Trevor, and Zach are on the team scheduled to play against us tomorrow!"

"Oh, Great!" said Connor. "Those are the three meanest guys at our school! What luck!"

"Yeah, and if we lose, we'll never hear the end of it," Matthew remarked.

Just then, Ronnie, Trevor, and Zach rounded the hall corner.

"Hey, Sport!" said Trevor, slapping Connor on the back. "I see we're playing ball against you tomorrow. What a joke! Your team has a bunch of wimps on it."

"We're gonna smear you," Ronnie added.

"You can't scare us," Connor said, trying to sound confident.

The three boys burst out laughing. "If you're smart, you won't even show up tomorrow," said Trevor.

With that, the boys sneered and continued walking down the hall.

Connor sighed. "We should practice more," he said.

"Well, it's too late to back out now!" said Matthew.

"You're right!" agreed Connor. "So let's give it our best shot!"

Before long, the big moment arrived.

When the Kids' Club members got to the baseball diamond, they saw many students already there.

The children laughed and chatted with other teammates while they waited for the game to begin.

Connor tied Rusty to the fence post and put a baseball cap on his head.

"Be a good mascot!" he said, giving his dog a pat.

The school coach, Mr. Jordan, told the teams to gather around. They flipped a coin and Connor's team won. They would bat first.

"All right!" said Connor.

He picked up a bat and walked toward the batter's box.

"This will be a seven-inning game," said Mr. Jordan. "Play ball!"

Connor and his friends soon realized they had a bigger problem than trying to win—Trevor, Ronnie, and Zach weren't playing fair!

Whenever Mr. Jordan wasn't looking, they cheated! Ronnie threw pitches at the batters, Zach tried to trip Matthew on the way to third base, and Trevor hit Lauren in the shoulder with a ball.

Connor complained to the coach, but the three boys denied they had done anything wrong.

As the game continued, the situation seemed to get worse. By the fifth inning, the Kids' Club team was losing six to three.

Connor's little brother, Ryan, stepped up to bat.

"Look at the little runt!" shouted Zach, "He can hardly hold a bat!"

Connor tried to encourage his brother. "Come on," he said. "You can do it!"

Ryan swung as hard as he could, but he missed the ball.

"Strike!" yelled the umpire, and Trevor laughed.

Ryan fanned the air again. "Strike two!" the umpire shouted.

"It's okay, Ryan," said Connor. "Keep your eye on the ball."

Ryan tried his best, but he failed for the third time.

"Three strikes, you're out!" yelled the umpire.

Trevor shouted from the outfield, "The little baby doesn't even know how to play baseball."

"Yeah," Zach added, "He's not even good enough for Pee Wee League."

"Hey!" Connor snapped. "Leave my brother alone!"

Trevor threw down his mitt and pushed up his sleeves.

"What are you going to do about it?" he asked.

"That's enough," said Mr. Jordan. "We're here to play baseball—not to have a fight."

"Sorry," apologized Connor as he stepped up to the plate.

Meanwhile, Rusty had broken free from the fence post. Connor didn't see his dog as he got ready to bat.

Connor swung and hit a fly ball that sent Rusty running across the field!

Trevor was all set to catch the ball, but Rusty jumped and grabbed it first, knocking Trevor flat on his back!

"Hey!" the boy shouted, dusting off his
jeans. "How did that dog get on the field?"
"Rusty belongs to me!" shouted Connor.
"That's an automatic out!" ordered the umpire.
Connor sighed as he sat down on the bench.
The remainder of the game was a complete disaster.

Ronnie, Zach, and Trevor continued to harass everyone, and the Kids' Club team never could make a comeback. The score was seven to three when the game ended. Connor and his friends had lost, just like Trevor and his friends had promised.

The three bullies laughed and made fun of the other team.

"Don't pay any attention," said Lauren. "Let's just go home."

Connor didn't have much to say as they walked toward Sunny Street. In fact, his mood didn't change for the rest of the night. He hardly ate any dinner, and he didn't even want to watch his favorite TV program.

The next morning, an unhappy Connor met his friends at Sunday school.

The teacher taught a lesson about learning from things that don't go the way we want. She quoted a Bible verse in Romans 8:28, *"We know that in everything God works for the good of those who love him."*

Connor was confused. "How can something work for good if you fail?" he asked.

"There are many ways," replied the teacher. "Remember that Abraham Lincoln, one of the greatest men in history, lost three elections before he became President."

"Wow!" said Connor. "I never knew that."

"It's true," said the teacher. "God can take difficulties and use them to make us stronger and wiser."

Connor felt a lot better after hearing what the teacher had to say.

When Sunday school was over, the children saw
Mr. Jordan in front of the church. They walked over to
say hello.

"Hi!" he said. "I know you felt bad about losing the
game yesterday, but I was still proud of all of you.
When the other team was being mean, you didn't try
to repay them. That took a lot of courage."

"Thanks," said Matthew. "But we lost the game."

That's not as important as character," said Mr. Jordan. "There are more important things than winning."

"Yeah, that's what my Sunday school teacher said," agreed Connor. "But it still would have felt good to win. We'll have to practice harder next time."

"And one more thing," laughed Mr. Jordan. "Leave Rusty at home! That dog has a *big* mouth!"